Plop!

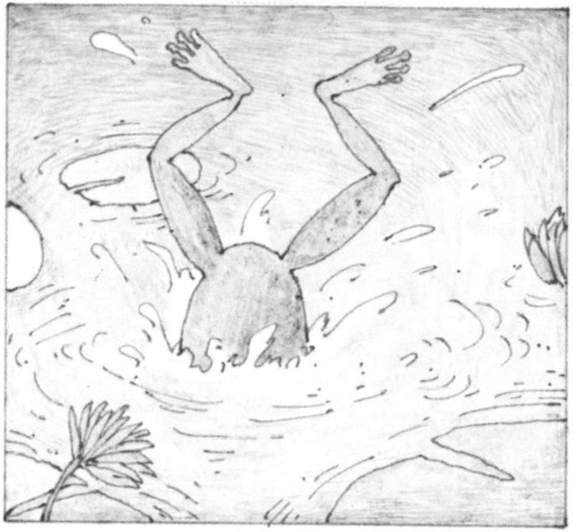

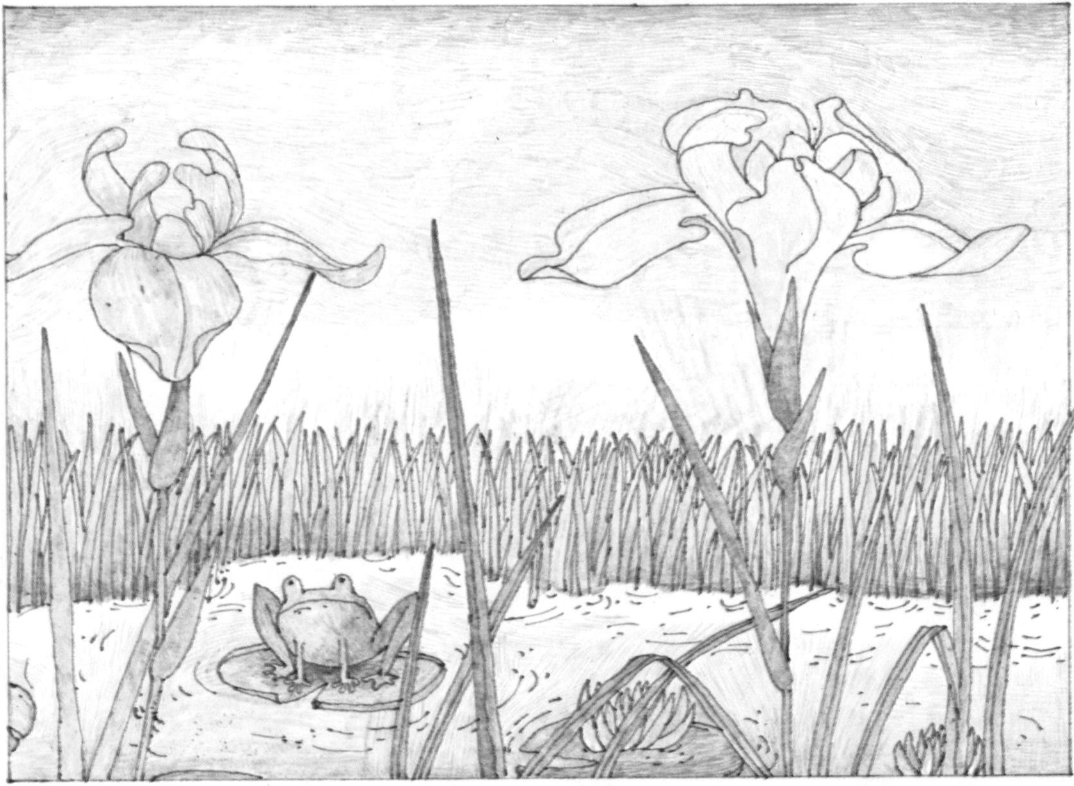

Little frog can see the flowers.

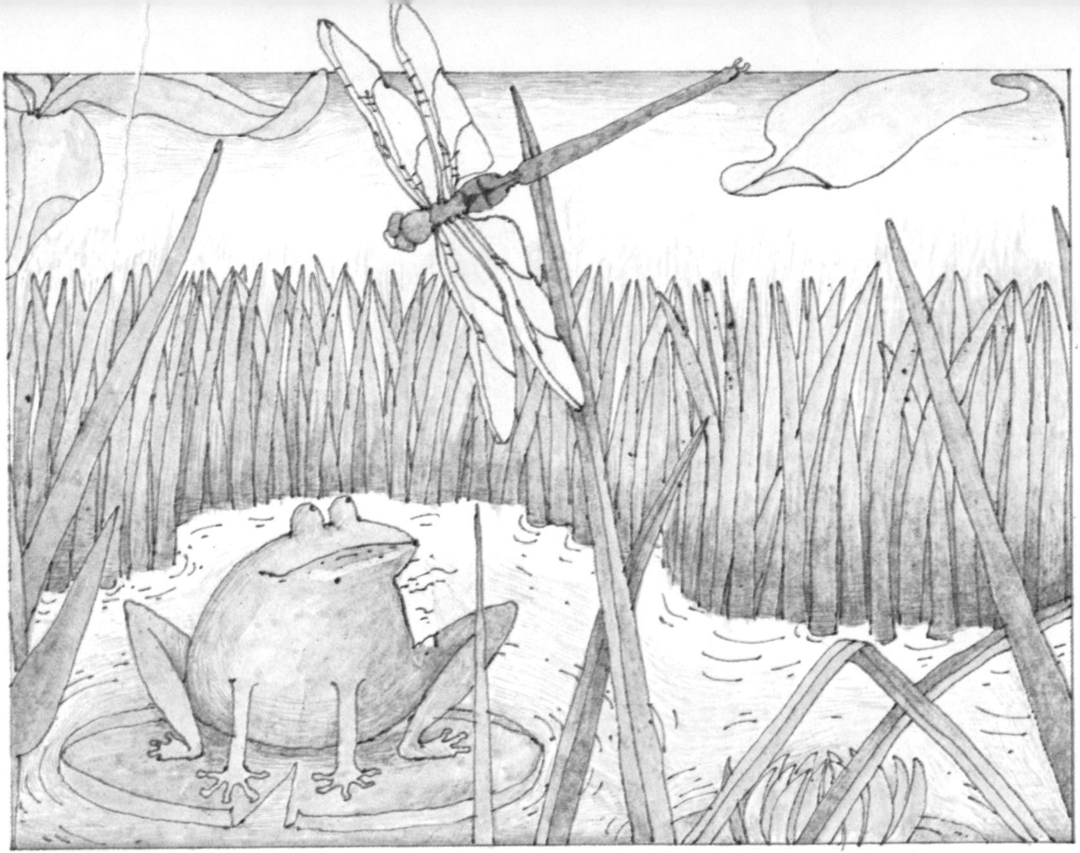

He can see the dragonfly.

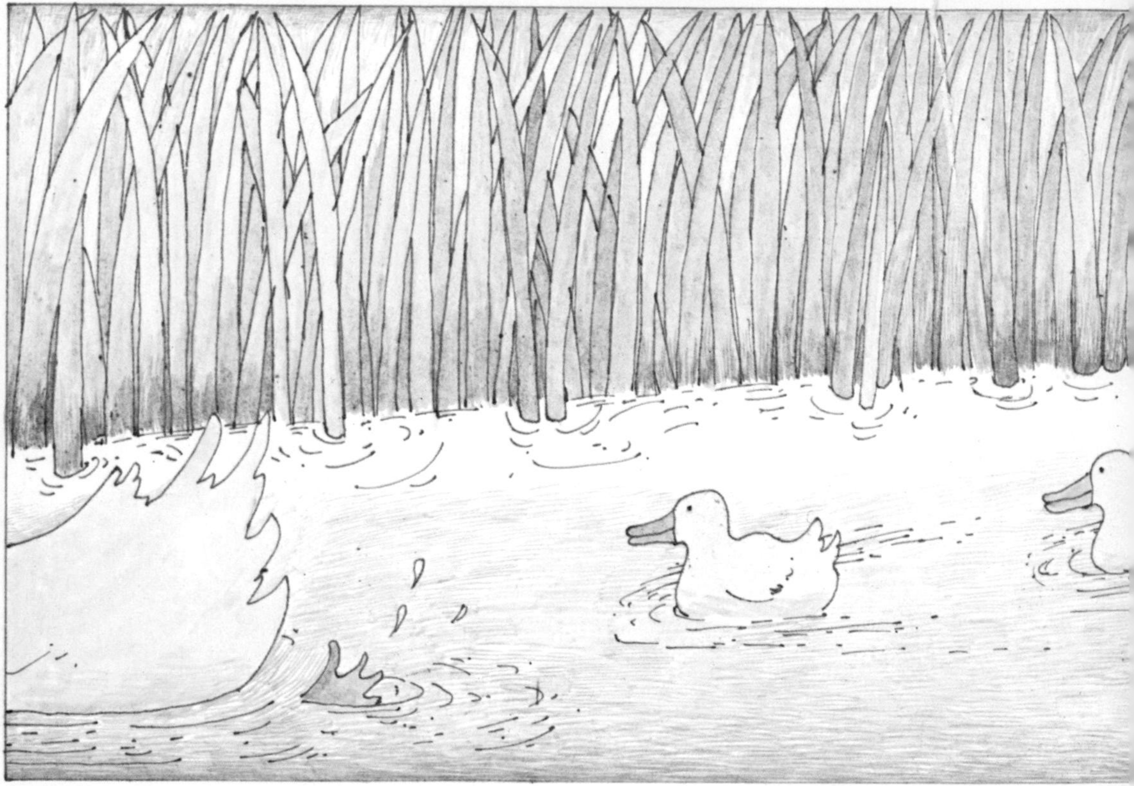

He can see

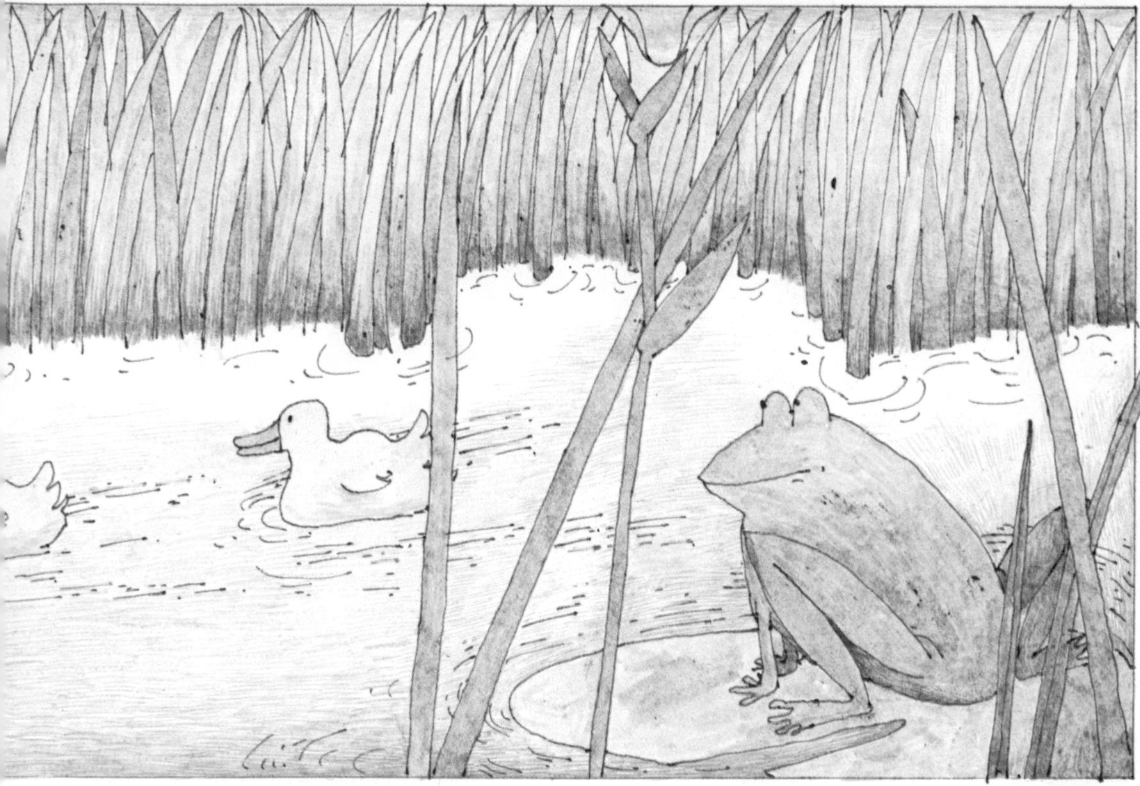

the ducklings.

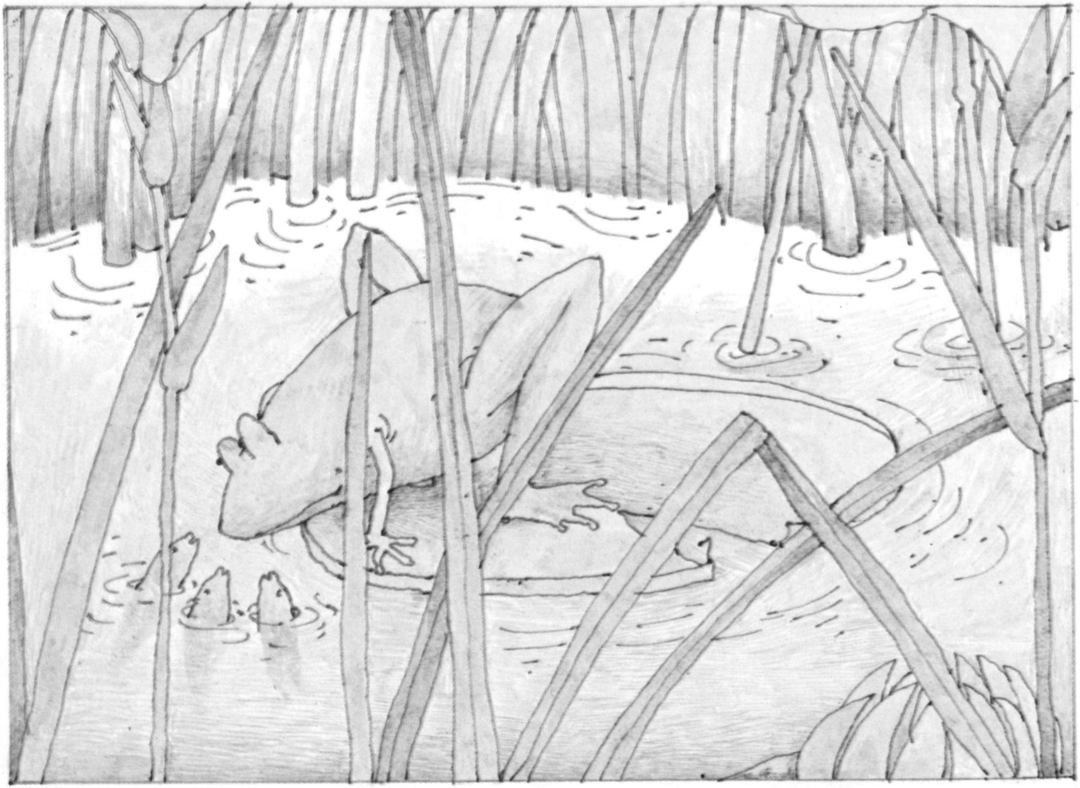

He can see the fish.

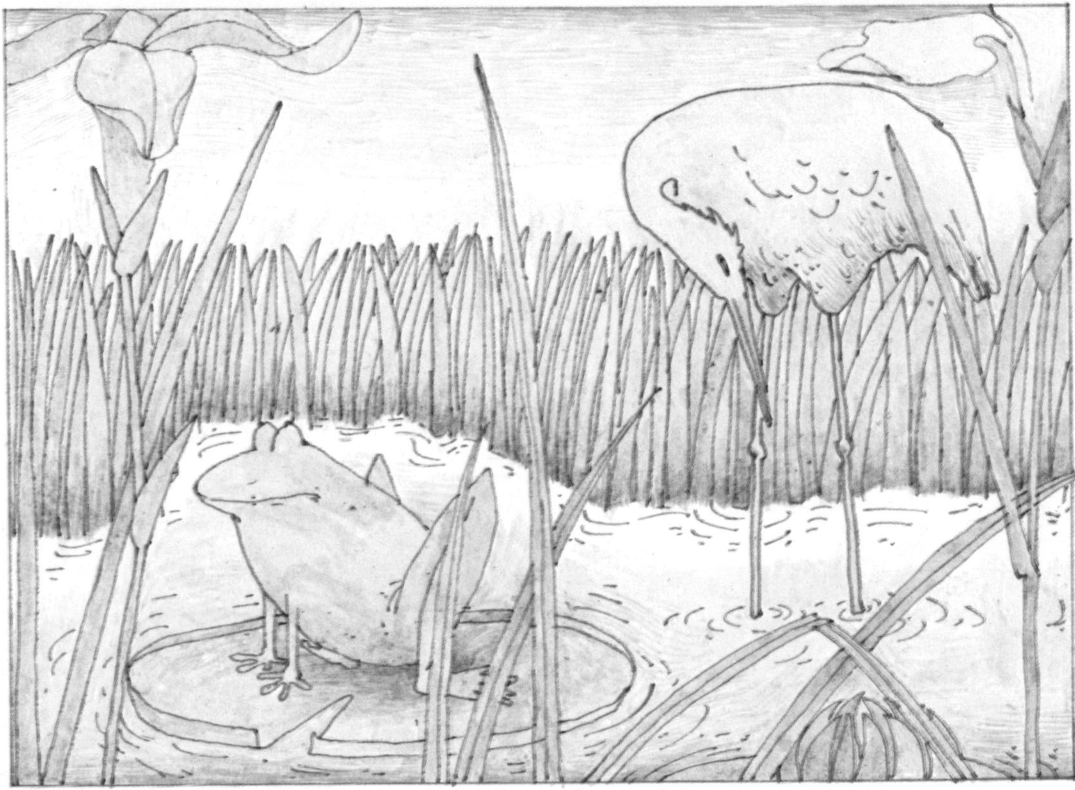

Can he see the big bird?

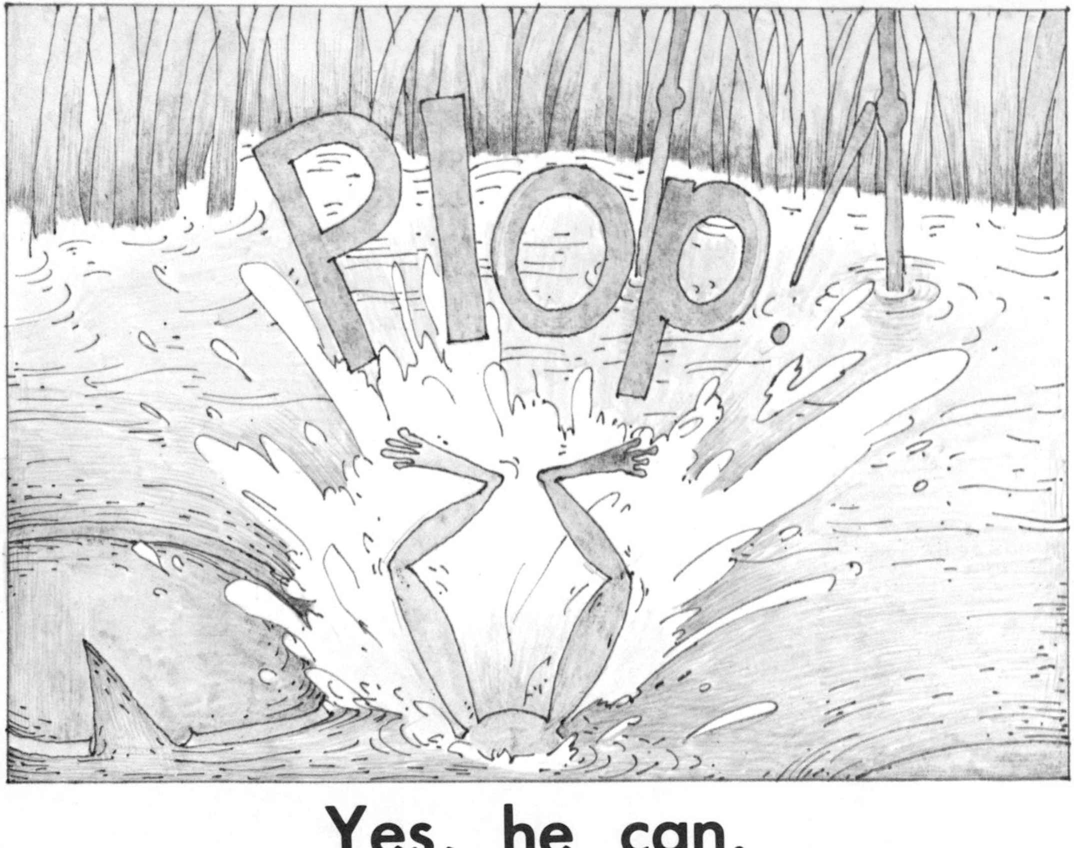

Yes, he can.